Lulu Bell and the

Moon Dragon

A Random House book
Published by Random House Australia Pty Ltd
Level 3, 100 Pacific Highway, North Sydney NSW 2060
www.randomhouse.com.au

First published by Random House Australia in 2013

Addresses for companies within the Random House Group can be found at
www.randomhouse.com.au/offices

National Library of Australia
Cataloguing-in-Publication Entry

Author: Murrell, Belinda
Title: Lulu Bell and the moon dragon/Belinda Murrell; Serena Geddes, illustrator
ISBN: 978 1 74275 881 7 (pbk.)
Series: Murrell, Belinda. Lulu Bell; 4
Target audience: For primary school age
Other authors/contributors: Geddes, Serena
Dewey number: A823.4

Cover and internal illustrations by Serena Geddes
Cover design by Christabella Designs
Internal design and typesetting in 16/22 pt Bembo by Anna Warren, Warren Ventures
Printed in Australia by Griffin Press, an accredited ISO AS/NZS 14001:2004
Environmental Management System printer

Random House Australia uses papers that are natural, renewable and recyclable
products and made from wood grown in sustainable forests. The logging and
manufacturing processes are expected to conform to the environmental regulations
of the country of origin.

Lulu Bell and the Moon Dragon

Belinda Murrell

Illustrated by Serena Geddes

RANDOM HOUSE AUSTRALIA

Molly   Tien and Sam   Lulu

Dad   Mum   Gus   Rosie

For sharing my first Autumn Moon Festival
with me – Rob, Nick, Emily and Lachie.
And for our fellow Vietnam adventurers,
Fi, Tim, Hamish and Charlie.

Chapter 1

The Moon Festival

It was Wednesday lunchtime. Lulu and her best friend Molly were sitting on a bench under a huge old tree in the school playground. All around them, kids were yelling and laughing and playing.

'Molly,' Lulu said, 'do you want to come over this afternoon to do some drawing?'

Molly looked excited, but then she frowned. She shook her head.

1

'Sorry, Lulu, I can't,' said Molly. 'Sam and I promised Mum we'd help her get ready for the Vietnamese Moon Festival. It's next Monday.'

Sam was Molly's younger brother.

'The Moon Festival?' asked Lulu. 'What's that?'

Molly opened her lunchbox and pulled out her container of noodle salad.

'When my mum was a little girl in Vietnam, the villagers would have a big Moon Festival every year. It was held to celebrate the end of the rice harvest,' explained Molly. 'It's a time for parents to have fun with their children.'

Molly stirred her noodles with her fork, mixing the vegetables through. Lulu took a big bite of her apple.

'It's always held in the middle of autumn, at the time of the eighth full moon,' said Molly. 'For Vietnamese children, it's the most exciting time of the year. It's like Christmas and Easter and Halloween all rolled into one!'

'That sounds fantastic,' said Lulu. 'But where will it be?' She took another bite of her apple.

'Mum thought we could have our own festival at home. We've never done it before,' said Molly. 'Usually children dress up as dragons, lions and fairy spirits. They parade through the streets, dancing and playing music. Afterwards they have a huge feast.'

Lulu smiled and her brown eyes sparkled. 'Wow,' she said. 'I'd love to see that.'

'Why don't you come over to my place this afternoon? You can help us get ready,' suggested Molly. 'Mum wants to start making the costumes. Then we'll make masks and paper lanterns. There's a lot to do.'

Lulu nodded and flicked one of her honey-blonde plaits over her shoulder. 'I'd love to,' she said. 'I'll ask Mum after school.'

Chapter 2

The Excursion

After lunch, the girls went back into class and sat at their desks. Their teacher Miss Baxter was wearing a wide straw hat. Lulu wondered why she had a hat on in class.

'Good afternoon, 3B,' said the teacher.

'Good afternoon, Miss Baxter,' chorused the students.

'Today we have a very special treat for you,' said Miss Baxter. She smiled around at the class. 'We have just had a call from one of the parents. She said there are two humpback whales swimming near Shelly Beach. So we are going on an excursion to visit them.'

There was a buzz of excited chatter among the children. Shelly Beach School was just a block from the ocean. The students often went on excursions to explore the rock pools, play games on the beach or build sand sculptures. But this was the first time they had been out to visit whales in the wild.

'We are going to take one of the kindy classes with us,' added Miss Baxter.

'I wonder if we will be going with Sam's class,' whispered Molly. Molly's brother Sam was in kindy.

Lulu shrugged.

Miss Baxter put a big bottle of

sunscreen on her desk. 'Now, let's get ready, 3B,' she said. 'Everyone needs to put on their hats and some sunscreen.'

The kids scrambled to slather on sunscreen. They collected their navy blue hats from their hooks in the corridor. Everyone was chattering loudly about the unexpected outing.

They lined up in a shady spot in the playground. The kindy students came out with their teacher, Miss Stevens. Molly's little brother Sam was standing on his own. He had spiky black hair that stood up on end, and thick glasses. He looked lost.

'Hi, Sam,' called Molly and Lulu together.

Sam smiled and came over.

'Are you having a good day?' asked Lulu.

'It's okay,' said Sam.

'I didn't see you at lunchtime,' said Molly.

'I was reading in the library,' Sam explained. 'It was too hot to play.'

Molly looked worried. 'Sam, you can't spend every lunchtime in the library. You need to get out and have fun with the other kids.'

Sam looked away. Lulu thought he seemed sad.

'There are lots of lovely kids in kindy,' said Lulu. 'You just need to get to know them.'

Sam smiled up at Lulu. He nodded.

Lulu and Molly were given the job of looking after Sam and a kindy girl called Hannah. The students lined up two by two to walk to the beach. Lulu walked with Sam, and Molly with Hannah. Miss Baxter and Miss Stevens led the group. Three parents had also volunteered to come along.

The lines of children headed out the school gate. They snaked down the footpath towards the ocean. Lulu could feel the sea breeze cooling her cheeks. She breathed in deeply.

The teachers held up the traffic while the students crossed the road. On the other side was a wide park above the beach. Cyclists whizzed past on bikes. Mums pushed babies in prams. Dogs trotted along, dragging their owners for a walk.

On the other side of the park was the sea.

The sun danced on the sparkling blue water. Close to the shore, pale green waves rolled and smashed onto the crumbly white sand. The air smelled of salt and seaweed.

'Where are the whales?' asked Lulu. She shaded her eyes. 'I can't see any.'

Miss Baxter pointed to the right.

'The whales are in the cove further along the foreshore,' she explained. 'But we may need to be patient. Did you know that humpback whales can hold their breath underwater for nearly an hour?'

'An hour!' exclaimed Lulu. 'I hope we don't have to wait that long.'

The students walked along the footpath around the foreshore. After a

few minutes, they came to a slight rise.
It was fenced off from the rocks below.
The children crowded around the fence
and looked down at the calm water.
Hannah started chatting to one of the
other girls in her class.

A group of kindy boys gathered
together. They leaned against the railings,
joking and laughing. One of the boys
looked over at Sam.

'Do you want to go and join your friends, Sam?' asked Molly.

Sam shook his head. 'No, it's okay,' he said. 'I'll stay here with you.'

Suddenly Molly pointed and cried out, 'Look!'

Lulu gazed out over the sea. A white splash caught her eye.

'Is that a whale?' asked Lulu.

Chapter 3

The Whales

A huge black-and-white whale leaped from the water. It arced through the air and then smashed down again with a loud splash.

'Wow,' called Lulu. 'Did you see that?'

'It's beautiful,' replied Molly.

A moment later, there were two whales leaping and diving. They whacked their tails and slapped their fins against the water. It was as though the two whales were putting on an acrobatic performance especially for the children.

'They are two young males,' explained Miss Baxter. 'The males practise breaching and diving so they can show off to the females.'

'Some human boys are just the same,' whispered Lulu. 'They like showing off to the girls too.'

Lulu and Molly giggled.

One of the whales shot a spout of water metres into the air.

'Do you see that spout?' asked Miss Stevens. 'Whales are mammals, just like humans. They breathe air in through their blowholes. When they breathe out, they force water out in a huge spout.'

The other male blew another spout even higher.

Both whales swam closer to the

shore. They swam on their sides with
their huge mouths open. They looked
as though they were laughing. Lulu and
Molly laughed too.

'They are like clowns at the circus,'
said Lulu. 'They seem to like us watching
them.'

'*Giant* clowns,' agreed Molly.

'Whales spend the summer months
down near the Antarctic,' said Miss
Baxter. 'They eat fish and tiny sea

animals called krill. In summer they can eat nearly a thousand kilograms of food in just one day.'

'Wow!' said Molly.

'No wonder they are so big,' said Lulu.

Miss Baxter smiled and said, 'They can weigh about thirty-six *thousand* kilograms. They don't eat that much all year round. In winter they hardly eat at all. That's when they live off their stored fat.'

Miss Baxter looked around at all the children. Sam stared at her with big serious eyes.

The whales breached again and then dived deep under the sea. When they surfaced they were much further from the shore.

'In autumn, the whales migrate up to the warm tropical waters. They have their babies there during winter,' said Miss Stevens. 'In spring, they migrate south again. Humpback whales can migrate more than twenty thousand kilometres in a year.'

'That's a lot of swimming,' said Molly.

The whales swam on their sides and waved their flippers. The children waved back. The whales dived again and disappeared.

'Oh no,' said Lulu. 'I think they've gone.'

The children waited patiently for
a few minutes but the whales were
nowhere to be seen. Sam edged closer
to the fence to get a better view of the
ocean.

One of the boys bumped against Sam
and grinned. Sam's glasses were knocked
sideways. He hurried back towards Lulu
and Molly.

'Who was that boy, Sam?' whispered
Lulu.

Sam shrugged as he straightened his glasses. 'Oh, just Oliver.'

'Is he one of your friends?' asked Molly.

Sam looked away. 'Not really,' he said.

Before Molly or Lulu could say anything else, Miss Baxter clapped her hands. 'Okay, children,' she called. 'Time to go back to school.'

'Ooooh,' groaned some of the children.

Lulu didn't mind. She loved being in Miss Baxter's class.

Chapter 4

A Plan

After school, Lulu's mum Chrissie was waiting with Lulu's younger brother Gus. Gus was wearing his favourite red-and-green superhero outfit. It had a black face mask, bobbly antennae and a green cloak that swirled as Gus ran.

'Hi, Lulu,' called Gus as he dashed past. He headed straight for the climbing frame. 'Bug Boy can fly . . .'

'Hi, Gussie,' called Lulu. 'Don't try to fly off the top!'

Molly's mum Tien was standing next to Mum, chatting. Lulu's younger sister Rosie and Molly's brother Sam came running up to join their mothers.

'Hi, Sam,' said Tien. 'Did you have a lovely day?'

'It was great,' said Sam. 'I went to see the whales with Molly and Lulu.'

'That's not fair,' complained Rosie. 'We didn't get to see the whales.'

Lulu and Molly described

their excursion to see the two humpback whales.

'You are so lucky to see whales in the wild,' said Mum. 'When I was growing up we never saw whales. They had been hunted nearly to extinction.'

Lulu felt sad to think that the beautiful whales had nearly been wiped out.

'Now they are protected, we see whales at Shelly Beach quite often,' said Mum.

Gus came swooping back, his cloak flying.

'Come on, Molly and Sam,' said Tien. 'We'd better get home. We have lots to do today.'

Molly picked up her schoolbag and swung it over her shoulder. 'Mum, can Lulu come over this afternoon and help

us get ready for the Moon Festival?' she asked.

Tien smiled at Molly and Lulu. 'Of course she can,' she said. 'I thought we could start making the dragon costume today.'

'Ooh, that sounds interesting,' said Mum. 'What is the Moon Festival?'

Tien told them all about the traditional Vietnamese event.

'In Vietnamese, we call it *Tet Trung Thu*,' said Tien. 'It was my favourite day of the year when I was growing up.'

Tien smiled at Molly and Lulu as she explained. 'Kids dress up as dragons, lions and mischievous fairy spirits and dance around the streets. They bang drums and clash cymbals to frighten away the evil spirits.'

'Oh, could I dress up as a fairy spirit?' asked Rosie.

She twirled around on her toes. Rosie's favourite outfit was her feathery angel wings with her white dress and sparkly thongs. Sometimes she even wore her wings with her school uniform.

'Would you all like to join us for the festival on Monday, Chrissie?' asked Tien. 'I thought it would be nice for Molly and Sam to experience a traditional

Vietnamese celebration. But it would be more fun with extra children.'

'It sounds like the most wonderful idea,' agreed Mum. 'Could we help you prepare for it?'

'That would be great,' said Tien. 'It's Wednesday today and there's lots to do. On Monday I thought the kids could dress up and parade down our street. Afterwards they could come back to our apartment for some mooncakes.'

Mum nodded. 'Or perhaps we could finish down at the beach and have a picnic there?'

'Oh, yes,' agreed Tien. 'Let's have a feast at the beach.'

It was agreed that the Bell family would join in. The two families walked home together, chatting about what needed to be done.

Chapter 5

Dragon Suit

Molly lived in a block of apartments. It was right next door to the Shelly Beach Vet Hospital, where Lulu and her family lived. Lulu's dad Dr Bell was a vet. The family had a wonderful collection of animals and pets.

The girls were greeted at the door by Molly's black kitten Ebony-Lou. Molly scooped her up and kissed her nose. Ebony-Lou purred loudly.

In the lounge room, Tien brought out lots of photos. Some showed children wearing traditional costumes to the festival.

Some children were dressed up in pairs as a dragon or a lion. One child was the head and the other child was the tail. The costumes were bright and colourful, in red, gold, yellow, white and silver.

'This character is called Ong Dia,' said Tien. She showed them a picture of a boy with a round, pink, smiling mask and blue robes. 'Ong Dia means Lord Earth.

It is Lord Earth who urges the dragon to fly and dance. I thought we'd make some masks like this.'

Lulu's mum nodded and said, 'They should be easy to make with papier-mâché and paint.' Lulu's mum was an artist. She had created the most wonderful costumes for Lulu, Rosie and Gus. She had made mermaids, angels, superheroes and even a King Neptune costume for Dad.

Some of Tien's photos showed graceful girls. They wore the traditional Vietnamese dress called *ao dai*. This was a long slim tunic worn over pantaloons. The girls had their faces painted. They carried lanterns shaped like stars, moons, butterflies and fish.

'I want to wear a costume like that,' said Rosie. 'It looks so beautiful.'

'You can borrow mine,' said Molly. 'My aunts sent me one from Vietnam for my birthday.'

'What will you wear then, Molly?' asked Lulu.

'I want to dress as a dragon and dance,' said Molly. 'I've always loved dragons in Vietnamese fairytales.'

'Is it hard to do a dragon dance?' asked Lulu. 'Could I be the dragon tail?'

Molly nodded, her black eyes shining. 'We can take it in turns to be the head.'

Everyone set to work. Tien had bought metres of shiny, coloured fabric. She also had silver and gold fringing, and a feathery white boa. Ebony-Lou pounced on the boa and rolled in it. She thought it was alive. In a moment the boa was a tangle of black kitten and white feathers.

The dragon needed big goggly red
eyes, sharp white teeth and a white beard.
Tien had already made the cardboard
face with a wide pink mouth. Lulu and
Molly started gluing on white feathers.

Tien was making a long red cloak
on her sewing machine. This would be
attached to the dragon's head. The cloak
would form the body and tail. Then
Tien would make two pairs of loose red
trousers for the legs. The back and legs
would be decorated with strips of gold
fringing.

'The dragon's beard is a bit crooked,' said Molly.

Lulu cocked her head to one side as she checked. 'Maybe,' said Lulu. 'I think he just needs more feathers. The one in the picture has furry eyebrows as well.'

Rosie and Sam blew up balloons to form a base for the papier-mâché masks. Gus played football with the floating balloons.

'Take that!' cried Gus. A balloon popped with a loud bang.

'Gussie!' said Lulu. She put her hands on her hips. 'Don't burst all the balloons.'

Mum looked up from the gluggy pot she was stirring.

'Why don't you come and help me with the papier-mâché, honey bun?' suggested Mum. She held up a strip of newspaper soaked in paste.

Mum had mixed up a big batch of flour and water to make the paste. She was placing sticky strips of newspaper over each of the balloons to form a round face mask.

Gus ran to help. He dunked a fistful of newspaper into the paste pot. In a few minutes he managed to get white paste all over his Bug Boy outfit.

Mum put the masks out to dry in the sun on the verandah. Then she helped Tien sew the blue robes to go with them.

At last, Lulu and Molly finished decorating the dragon head. They packed up the glue, scissors and decorations. Mum folded up the last blue robe.

'That was fun,' said Mum. 'But now we need to go home and feed all the animals. It's nearly dinnertime.'

'We can paint the masks and make some lanterns tomorrow,' said Tien. 'Then over the weekend we can prepare some food so it's all ready for Monday.'

'It's my news day tomorrow,' said Lulu. 'Can Molly and I take the dragon costume in to show our class? The kids would love to see him.'

Mum frowned. 'I don't think so, Lulu,' said Mum. 'We don't want him to get damaged. Perhaps we could make a practise lantern tonight after dinner? You could take that for news instead?'

'Good idea. Thanks Mum.'

Lulu held up the colourful dragon head. She swooped the dragon gently through the air, making him fly. The red cloak billowed out behind him.

'He looks quite ferocious, honey bun,' said Mum.

'He looks awesome,' replied Lulu. She and Molly grinned at one another. 'I can't wait until Monday.'

Chapter 6

Four Eyes

The next day at recess, Lulu was walking through the playground. She heard a small voice calling her name. It was Molly's brother Sam.

'Lulu,' called Sam. 'Lulu Bell.'

Sam's hair was sticking up more than usual. His dark eyes blinked behind his thick, black-rimmed glasses.

'Hi, Sam,' replied Lulu. 'What's up?'

Sam frowned. 'Lulu, I'm . . . I'm not

very happy. And I can't find Molly.'

'Molly had to take a message to the office for our teacher,' said Lulu. 'But why aren't you happy, Sam?'

Sam looked over his shoulder towards the monkey bars. Most of the kindy kids were swinging back and forth on the bars.

'One of the boys was mean to me,' said Sam. He blinked away tears.

'Oh, Sam. I'm sorry,' said Lulu. She kneeled down and gave him a hug. 'What happened?'

Sam sniffed. He took off his glasses and rubbed his eyes.

'He called me Four Eyes,' said Sam. 'Because of my glasses.'

Lulu frowned. She hated it when kids teased other kids.

'That's not very nice,' said Lulu. 'He shouldn't call you mean names.'

Lulu thought for a moment. *What should she do? How could she best help Sam?*

'Have you told your teacher?' asked Lulu.

Sam shook his head. 'No. I was too scared.'

Lulu stood up and flicked one of her honey-blonde plaits over her shoulder.

'Come with me, Sam,' said Lulu. 'Let's go and find Miss Stevens.'

Sam hesitated. Lulu smiled at him.

'Miss Stevens is lovely,' Lulu reassured him. 'You don't need to be scared of telling her. She'll know what to do.'

Lulu and Sam walked towards the kindy classroom.

'Who was the boy who called you names?' asked Lulu.

'Oliver,' replied Sam.

Lulu remembered Oliver from the day before. He was the blond boy who had bumped Sam near the fence.

'Well, Sam,' said Lulu. 'You tell Oliver that you have a big sister called Molly. *And* you have an eight-year-old friend called Lulu. We don't like you being teased. So if he calls you names again, we'll come and look after you.'

Sam smiled up at Lulu. 'Thanks, Lulu,' he said.

Miss Stevens was sitting at her desk in the classroom. Brightly coloured artwork hung on the walls. In the corner in a glass tank was a mouse called Archie.

The brown-and-white mouse was running on his exercise wheel, making it spin.

'Hello, Lulu,' said Miss Stevens. 'Hello, Sam. Is everything all right?'

Sam hung his head.

'Do you want to tell Miss Stevens what happened, Sam?' asked Lulu.

Sam shook his head.

'Shall I tell her?'

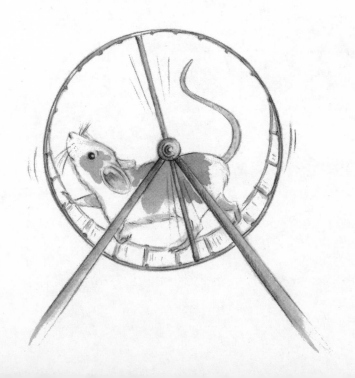

Sam nodded.

'Miss Stevens, Sam is a bit upset,'
explained Lulu. 'Oliver called him names.'

Miss Stevens smiled at Sam and then
at Lulu.

'Thanks for your help, Lulu,' said Miss
Stevens. 'You are very kind. I'll go and
have a little chat with Oliver. Perhaps

I need to remind him that in KS we are always caring to one another.'

Sam beamed at Miss Stevens and then at Lulu.

'Thanks, Lulu,' he whispered. 'I feel better now.'

Lulu felt a glow of warmth.

'It's my pleasure, Sam,' replied Lulu. 'Remember to come and see me if you need any more help.'

Chapter 7

Star Lanterns

After recess it was news time.

Lulu went last. She had brought in
the practice lantern that she and Mum
had created the night before. It was
made of crimson paper, with purple satin
ribbons. Lulu had cut out lots of tiny
stars for the light to shine through. It
dangled from a long dowel rod.

That morning, Lulu had asked Molly
if she wanted to tell the class about the

festival. Molly had shaken her head. It wasn't her turn and she didn't like news time as much as Lulu did.

So Lulu stood in front of the class and talked about her lantern.

'On Monday it will be the full moon,' explained Lulu. 'Our family wants to help Molly celebrate by dressing up in traditional Vietnamese costumes. We've never been to a Moon Festival before.'

Miss Baxter picked up the lantern and examined it carefully.

'It's beautiful. You don't put a candle inside it, do you?' asked Miss Baxter. 'That might be quite dangerous. The lantern could catch on fire.'

'No,' said Lulu. 'In the olden days, they used real candles. But Mum thought we should use a battery-powered candle.'

'That sounds fantastic, Lulu,' said Miss Baxter. 'Thank you for telling us about your star lantern and the dragon costume.'

Miss Baxter turned to Molly. 'I know it's not your news day today, Molly,'

said the teacher, 'but I wonder if you could tell us a little more about the Moon Festival?'

Molly was often shy when she had to speak in front of the class. She didn't like to be the centre of attention.

Molly stood up slowly. She glanced at Lulu as though begging for help. Lulu gave her a thumbs-up to give her courage.

Molly paused. 'Um. Well . . .'

Miss Baxter nodded and smiled. Molly started to explain the Moon Festival to the class. Once she started talking she forgot to be nervous.

'When we've finished painting the masks we still have to make more lanterns,' said Molly. 'Then we'll bake lots of mooncakes to eat.'

'That's a lot of preparation,' said Miss Baxter. 'I have a very good idea. For craft this afternoon, the whole class is going to make Vietnamese lanterns.'

Molly smiled with pride. Lulu grinned back.

'Do you think you could help us, Molly and Lulu?' asked Miss Baxter. 'We might need some artistic direction.'

'Sure,' said Molly and Lulu together.

After lunch, the whole class set to

work. Lulu and Molly chose the materials from the craft cupboard. There was paper and cardboard in lots of bright colours – red, pink, purple, yellow and white. They fetched scissors, sticky tape, staplers, ribbon and special hole punchers.

First, each student decorated a sheet of coloured paper. They cut out star or moon shapes with the hole punchers.

'Once you've decorated the paper,' explained Lulu, 'you need to roll the paper into a tube and sticky-tape it.'

Molly showed the class how to make the base from a circle of cardboard. The base was firmly sticky-taped to the paper tube. Coloured ribbon was stapled to the top of the lantern to form a handle. The lantern could be carried by this ribbon handle or tied to a long dowel rod.

Miss Stevens came in during the class to ask Miss Baxter a question. She smiled when she saw the students all busily working.

'Our class is making lanterns,' explained Miss Baxter. 'It's the Vietnamese Moon Festival next week. Molly and Lulu have been telling us all about it.'

Miss Stevens nodded and rubbed her chin. She glanced at Lulu and then at Molly.

'Molly, you're Sam's big sister, aren't you?' asked Miss Stevens.

Molly nodded.

'I have an idea,' Miss Stevens said to Miss Baxter. 'Could I borrow Lulu and Molly for a little while, please?'

Lulu was surprised. *What could Miss Stevens want them to do?*

Chapter 8

The Fairy and the Dragon

 Lulu and Molly followed Miss Stevens into the kindy classroom. The children had been reading in groups with parent helpers. The parents were just packing up the readers while the students returned to their desks.

'Now KS,' began Miss Stevens, 'we have two very special guests in our classroom today. Molly is Sam's big sister and Lulu is their friend. I have asked Lulu and Molly to talk to us about an important celebration, which is happening next week.'

The kindy children looked at the girls, then at Sam. Lulu and Molly glanced at each other in surprise.

The Moon Festival is certainly creating a lot of interest, thought Lulu.

Molly and Lulu talked about the festival and the costumes they had made. Several of the parents stayed to listen.

'I wondered if you might be able to tell us anything else about dragons, Molly?' asked Miss Stevens.

Molly thought for a moment.

'What about the story of how the Vietnamese people were born?' suggested

Sam. He peered at Molly through his round glasses.

'Good idea, Sam,' said Molly.

Molly looked around at all the students. Lulu sat down on a spare seat. She had never heard Molly tell this story before.

'Many thousands of years ago,' began Molly, 'there was a powerful dragon king called Lac Long Quan. "*Long*" means "dragon" in Vietnamese.'

The kindy students all sat up straighter and listened carefully.

'The mighty sea dragon fell in love with a beautiful fairy princess called Au Co,' explained Molly. 'The fairy princess lived in the mountains with her fairy family. The sea dragon lived in a vast underwater palace.'

Lulu imagined a beautiful underwater palace built of coral and pearls.

'The sea dragon king transformed himself into human form. He tried to woo the fairy princess,' continued Molly. 'She fell in love with him and they were happily married. A year later, the fairy laid one hundred eggs.'

The kindy children giggled at the thought of a fairy princess laying eggs. Lulu giggled too.

'Then the eggs hatched,' said Molly.

'Out popped one hundred human babies.'

The children all laughed. Lulu
noticed that Sam was sitting next to
Oliver, the boy who had teased him.
Oliver leaned over and whispered
something to Sam. Sam grinned.

'The problem was that the dragon
king lived in his underwater palace.

The fairy had to live on land,' said Molly.
'She became lonely and homesick.
Queen Au Co longed to return to the
mountains where she had grown up.

'In the end, half their children stayed
with their father living by the sea,' said

Molly. 'The other half returned to the mountains with their mother. These one hundred children became the first people of Vietnam.'

Molly looked around at the attentive kindy children.

'So, all the Vietnamese people are like brothers and sisters,' explained Molly. 'Some live in the mountains and some live by the sea. But they are all descended from the dragon king and the fairy princess.'

Molly smiled. Everyone clapped. A few of the children leaned over to whisper to Sam. Sam nodded and sat up proudly.

'Thank you so much, Molly and Lulu,' said Miss Stevens. 'I think our class might make some lanterns next week as well.'

The parents stood up to leave.

'That was a lovely story,' said one of the mothers. 'When is your Moon Festival happening?'

'On Monday,' replied Molly.

The girls walked back to their own classroom.

'You told that story really well,' said Lulu. 'Sam was so proud of you. I think even Oliver was being nice to him.'

Molly smiled. 'Thanks, Lulu. It's easier to talk in front of people when you are excited about something.'

Chapter 9

Mooncakes

Finally it was Monday afternoon – the day of the full moon. It had rained during recess. And during lunchtime. Lulu had been frightened that the weather would be terrible all day and ruin the Moon Festival.

But in the afternoon, the clouds lifted and the sun came out.

Lulu went to Molly's house to help bake a huge batch of mooncakes for the feast.

Sam proudly showed Lulu his lantern on its bamboo pole. It was decorated with moons and dragons. Sam had drawn the fiery dragons, cut them out and stuck them on with glue.

'We made them in class today,' explained Sam. 'Everyone made one.'

'I love the dragons,' said Lulu. 'Your lantern's really cool.'

Molly's mother Tien had been making food all day in the tiny kitchen.

'I had a few phone calls today,' said Tien. She sounded puzzled. 'Some mothers from school rang and asked me about the Moon Festival. They were curious about where we were going.'

Lulu and Molly exchanged a glance.

'I told them we were starting here and walking down to the beach to have our picnic. I don't know how they all knew about it,' Tien finished.

'It must be because we talked about it at school last week,' suggested Molly.

'Maybe we'd better make some extra mooncakes,' said Tien. 'Just in case someone drops by to watch.'

Tien gave the girls a simple recipe to follow.

'The mooncakes my grandmother used to make were very complicated,' explained Tien. 'They took a month to prepare. Each one had a salty yolk in the centre to represent the full moon.'

'A whole month?' repeated Lulu. 'Didn't they go off?'

Tien picked up an egg and rolled it between her fingers.

'The eggs had to be salted for twenty-eight days – a full lunar cycle,' she explained. 'The salt preserved them. Then the cooking took a whole day. This is a much simpler and sweeter recipe. I think you'll like it.'

Lulu read the recipe. It did sound more delicious than salty eggs.

The girls stirred butter, sugar and egg yolks in a large bowl. Then Lulu added the flour and mixed it to make a rich dough.

Molly popped the dough in the fridge for half an hour. When it was chilled, Lulu and Molly rolled spoonfuls of dough in their hands to make round balls.

The final step was to stick their thumb in the middle to make a hole. This was filled with strawberry jam.

'This time last year, Mum made us mooncakes with red bean paste,' said Molly. 'But this year we thought some of the kids might prefer jam.'

At last, the girls finished making several trays of round mooncakes.

Tien popped the trays in the oven to cook. The kitchen filled with the delicious sweet smell of baking pastry.

When the cakes were golden brown, Tien pulled them out of the oven. She put them on a rack to cool.

'Yummo,' cried Lulu. 'They smell delicious.'

Just then the doorbell rang. Molly opened the door to let in Lulu's mum, Rosie and Gus. As usual, Gus was wearing his Bug Boy outfit.

Mum was carrying a big basket filled with goodies for the feast. She was wearing a long green Vietnamese-style dress over loose-fitting trousers. She had made them herself. Her long blonde hair hung down her back. The finishing touch was a conical cardboard hat. It was tied on with a wide green ribbon.

'Something smells delicious,' said Mum. She put the basket down on the table. 'You girls had better get dressed. It's nearly time to go.'

Lulu felt a shiver of excitement.

Rosie was already dressed in Molly's *ao dai*. It was a long, slim tunic of crimson silk over white pantaloons. Mum had painted Rosie's face with swirling black lines and red patterns. She had copied the design from one of Tien's photographs. Rosie looked completely different from her usual self.

Except, of course, she wore her feathery white angel wings. Lulu laughed when she saw them.

'I don't think Vietnamese fairies wear wings, Rosie,' said Lulu. 'At least they didn't in the photos we saw.'

Rosie pulled a disgusted face. She

66

fluttered around like a dainty red bird.

'Whoever heard of a fairy with no wings?' asked Rosie. 'I couldn't possibly go without wings.'

Sam emerged from his bedroom. He had changed from his school uniform and was wearing a long blue robe. Over his face he had a bright-pink smiley face mask. He carried a red drum and a pair of cymbals.

'Are you sure you don't want to dress up as Lord Earth, honey bun?' Mum asked Gus. 'I made you a lovely mask.'

'I not Lord Earth,' insisted Gus in disgust. 'I Bug Boy.'

Sam began to bang on his red drum. He danced around the room, his round mask grinning. The room filled with the pounding, thumping noise.

Gus grinned. He grabbed another

pink mask from the table and slipped it over his face. He picked up the cymbals and banged them together. *Clash. Crash. Clang.*

'I Moonface,' shouted Gus.

Lulu held her hands over her ears. 'Gussie. Not so loud.'

Mum gently took the cymbals and put them on the table.

'We might save the cymbals for outside, honey bun,' suggested Mum. 'We don't want to frighten the spirits away just yet.'

Tien came back. She had slipped away to change into her own dark blue *ao dai* dress. She looked delicate and pretty in the traditional costume. She wore a conical straw hat over her straight black hair.

Now only Lulu and Molly needed to get dressed up. The two girls slipped on their red–and–gold dragon trousers over their leggings.

Molly pulled on the dragon head. Her black eyes peered through the holes in the mask. Lulu lifted up the red cloak and disappeared underneath it. She grasped Molly around the waist and bent over.

The two girls were transformed into

a ferocious, fiery dragon. Lulu and Molly capered and danced. They had practised over the weekend. Now they could move as one creature.

Rosie laughed and clapped her hands. 'You look wonderful,' she cried.

'Let's go, honey buns,' said Mum.

'Yes, let the Moon Festival begin!' Tien cried.

Chapter 10

The Moon Festival

Asha and Jessie were tied up and waiting in Molly's front garden. The two dogs barked with excitement as Lulu and the group emerged from the building.

The dogs were very confused by the crimson creature that capered and cavorted in front of them. Then they had a good sniff and realised that it was just Lulu and Molly in disguise.

Rosie had dressed the dogs up too.

Both dogs wore pink tutus and fairy wings. They didn't mind. They were used to Rosie's games.

Parked next to the dogs was the big double pram. Mum stacked it high with containers of food.

'Let's go and see if Dad has finished work yet,' suggested Mum. 'He won't want to miss this for the world!'

Next door was the Shelly Beach Veterinary Hospital. The dragon pushed open the door with one clawed paw. The creature shook its head and roared. It was followed by two moon-faced imps carrying instruments. They crashed and clanged. Last of all came a Vietnamese fairy in a red gown.

Kylie, the vet nurse, was sitting behind the counter in the waiting room.

'Oh, hello,' said Kylie. 'Is that you in

there, Lulu? Hi, Rosie. Hi, Gus.'

'I not Gus,' shouted one of the imps. 'I Moonface.'

'Hello, Moonface.'

Lulu popped her head out from under the dragon costume. Her face was pink and her honey-blonde plaits were damp from dancing in the heavy costume. 'Hi, Kylie. Is Dad finished?'

'Your dad is just washing his hands,' Kylie assured her. 'He'll be right out. I'm going to lock up tonight.'

Dr Bell appeared at that moment. He was wearing his usual work clothes of a stripy blue-and-white shirt, fawn trousers and riding boots.

'Hello, monsters,' called Dr Bell. 'I'm ready to go. Thanks so much for locking up, Kylie.'

He swooped Rosie, then Gus, then Lulu up in the air one by one.

'Hi, Dad,' they chorused.

The group romped outside.

'You can't go like that,' said Mum. She had a cheeky glint in her eye. Dad held up his hand. He wore a look of mock horror on his face.

'Oh, no you don't, Chrissie,' he cried. 'I just happen to have a set of very

fine robes for you, right here,' said Mum.
She patted a parcel on top of the pram.

With a great flourish, Mum pulled
out a long blue robe and a conical hat
made of cardboard.

'Oh, no,' groaned Dad. 'Not again!'

'Yes, Dad,' insisted Lulu and Rosie
together. Mum flung the robe around
Dad's shoulders and popped the hat on
his head.

'At least there isn't a beard this time,' said Dad. He was referring to Rosie's mermaid birthday party. Mum had dressed him up as King Neptune.

'I nearly forgot!' said Mum. She pulled out a long, wispy beard made of

cotton wool. Dad laughed.

The two families set off down the road towards the beach. Cars tooted as they past. Pedestrians waved.

At the shops, a group of children were wearing cloaks and robes. They all carried lanterns. Some had drums or cymbals or clapping sticks. Some even carried saucepans, which they banged with wooden spoons.

'Hi, Lulu. Hi, Molly. Hello, Rosie. Hey, Sam,' called various voices.

'We've come to join the Moon Festival parade,' explained one tall boy.

Mum handed out some more round pink masks.

'It's lovely to see you,' said Tien. 'Please come and join us.'

Molly and Lulu capered and roared with delight. Sam banged his drum. Gus clanged his cymbals. The noisy parade continued towards the beach.

Another group of children waited for them at the traffic lights. Their parents stood back to watch. They smiled at the sight of the children in their colourful costumes.

Tien looked around. Her eyes filled with tears.

'Oh, my goodness,' she said. 'All these children have come to celebrate with us!'

Chapter 11

Lanterns and Moonlight

The children in the parade sang and danced and played their musical instruments. At last they reached the park at the beach. There was a huge crowd of children, parents and teachers waiting there. Miss Baxter and Miss Stevens waved.

The sun was setting in the west. The sky was streaked with rose-pink, apricot and violet. As the sun set, the children

79

switched on the electric candles in their
lanterns. Crimson, yellow, pink, orange
and white lanterns bobbed among the
crowd.

Molly lifted the dragon mask from

her shoulders. 'Your turn to be the head,' she said to Lulu.

'Are you sure?' asked Lulu.

'My arms are getting tired,' explained Molly. 'The dragon head gets a bit heavy after a while.'

So Lulu and Molly swapped. Lulu
had fun peering through the eyes of
the dragon mask. The dragon swooped
and soared among the lanterns. Parents
laughed and took photographs. Lulu felt
as if she was really flying.

'I *love* being a moon dragon,' cried
Lulu.

'Come and eat, honey buns,' called
Mum.

Lulu tucked the dragon head under
her arm.

Tien gestured to the feast laid out on
the picnic rug.

'In Vietnam, the dancers and
performers are always rewarded with
delicious food to eat,' said Tien. 'Here's
your reward.'

Tien had made platters of spring rolls
and pork dumplings and grilled chicken

skewers. Mum had made containers
of sliced tropical fruit – pineapple,
watermelon, mango, lychees and dragon
fruit. Then there were mounds of golden
mooncakes.

Other parents had brought food to share as well.

Gus was munching on a huge slice of watermelon. His pink mask was pushed back on top of his head.

'*Dulishus,*' said Gus. '*Waterlemon.* Moonface love *waterlemon.*'

'It's watermelon, Gussie,' Lulu corrected him.

'*Mmmmm, waterlemon,*' agreed Gus.

'He's *so* adorable,' cooed Mum.

'I not '*dorable,*' insisted Gus. His mouth was full of pink fruit. 'I imp.'

Lulu bit into one of the mooncakes. It was crumbly and sweet.

'Look, Molly,' cried Lulu. She pointed out to sea. A huge golden moon was rising slowly in the east. It was the biggest moon Lulu had ever seen.

'The full harvest moon,' replied Molly.

As the moon rose, it cast a glittering reflection across the ocean. It looked like a golden bridge across the sea.

Sam came running up. He was surrounded by a group of kindy boys. Several of them wore round pink Ong Dia masks. All of them carried a musical instrument of some sort. They pounded and shook them with glee.

'Where are the mooncakes?' called Sam. He tapped out a rhythm on his drum.

'Here they are, Sam,' offered Lulu. She picked up a bowl and handed it to him.

'You have to try these,' said Sam to the other boys. 'Mooncakes are the best.'

'Thanks, Sam,' cried several of the boys.

They pushed back their masks and each took a cake. They munched happily.

'These are great, Sam,' said a blond-haired boy. Lulu suddenly realised that it was Oliver. He was the boy who had called Sam names.

'Thanks, Oliver,' said Sam.

'Do you want to play handball with us tomorrow before school?' asked Oliver.

Sam blinked at Oliver through his

glasses. He gave an extra-big grin. 'That would be cool,' he said.

'Good,' said Oliver. 'Now, let's go and frighten away some more spirits.'

The boys ran off, pounding and banging and shaking their instruments.

Lulu smiled at Molly. 'It looks like Sam has made some friends,' said Lulu.

'Finally!' replied Molly.

Lulu gazed out to sea. The golden moon had risen higher.

A black shape crossed the moon's reflection in the water.

'Look who has come along to help celebrate the Moon Festival,' cried Lulu.

'Who?' asked Molly.

Lulu pointed out to the ocean. Under the round golden moon, two black whales were breaching and splashing.

'The whales,' cried Lulu.

Molly flung her arm around her best friend's shoulder. 'Perfect. This has been the *best* festival ever.'

Lulu Bell and the Cubby Fort

Lulu and her family are visiting their uncle's farm for the Easter holidays. There are horses to ride, a creek to swim in, and they can even sleep outside in a tent. What fun!

Lulu loves being a cowgirl on the farm, especially when all the cousins decide to build the best cubby fort ever. But when she sees a calf get stuck in the mud, Lulu has to find help – fast!

Out now

Read all the Lulu Bell books

Lulu Bell and the Birthday Unicorn

Lulu Bell and the Fairy Penguin

Lulu Bell and the Cubby Fort

Lulu Bell and the Moon Dragon

Lulu Bell and the Circus Pup

January 2014

Lulu Bell and the Sea Turtle

January 2014